THE ADVENTURES OF
CÚCHULAINN

THE ADVENTURES
OF
CÚCHULAINN

BAIRBRE MCCARTHY

MERCIER PRESS

MERCIER PRESS
5 French Church Street, Cork
16 Hume Street, Dublin 2

Trade enquiries to CMD DISTRIBUTION,
55a Spruce Avenue, Stillorgan Industrial Park, Blackrock, Dublin

ISBN 1 85635 312 5

10 9 8 7 6 5 4 3 2 1

FOR MY FATHER, CHRISTOPHER MCCARTHY

Printed in Ireland by Colour Books Ltd.

CONTENTS

The Birth of Setanta

King Conor's court at Eamhain Macha was always a hub of activity. Children of nobles flocked through the fort on their way to a game of hurling on the green or, later, laughing, they ran through the halls on their way to the druid's room to continue their lessons.

The druid, Cathbad, was a cranky, old man, but he told the most wonderful stories and kept the children under his spell. The king himself had explained to the children that Cathbad was suffering from the loss of his daughter. The beautiful Dechtera had disappeared from the court one day, several years before, and although the search for her was long and intense, she had never been found. There was much talk and speculation as to where the girl could be. She was a dreamy sort and none seemed to think her dead, just lost somewhere far away.

Sometimes, as the children entered the druid's room, they found him talking aloud to himself: 'If I only knew where you were, my child, I could bear this separation, if I knew you were well.'

One day when the children noisily clambered

into the room, the old man awoke from his reverie. Immediately, Cathbad began to tell the story of the last battle between the Tuatha Dé Danann and the Fomorian giants. This was a great favourite with the children who loved the beautiful, magical people of the goddess Dana and always enjoyed hearing of their triumphs over the ugly one-eyed giants. The great god Lugh, although just a boy, killed Balor, the leader of the giants with his sling shot and saved his people from the giants' tyranny. The children cheered when they heard that Lugh became the leader of the Tuatha Dé Danann.

Just then, shouts were heard outside in the orchard. Cathbad paused just long enough for the boys to become aware of the outdoor sounds. They rushed to the window and pushed for a view.

'Look, oh look. Have you ever seen such birds!' they exclaimed.

The birds were huge and colourful and had descended on the apple trees and were devouring the apples. King Conor came rushing from the fort calling his men. Fergus Mac Roy and many more of the Red Branch warriors ran out to chase the birds from the orchard. The birds flew away when the men chased them, but landed again not far away and continued to eat the crops.

All day long, the warriors followed them. Before they knew it, night had fallen and they were far from the fort, by the banks of the magical River Boyne.

They decided to stop there and rest for the night, as it was too dark to return to Eamhain Macha. They gathered wood and lit a fire for warmth. Then they lay down to sleep on the grass, wrapped in their cloaks.

Fergus Mac Roy found that the full moon was shining in his eyes and he could not sleep. He tossed and turned for a while, then decided to abandon this attempt at sleep. He arose and went for a walk by the river. It was a beautiful, star-lit night and he followed a grassy path until suddenly he saw before him a large pillared palace, blazing with the light of torches.

As he approached, he saw a wide marble staircase leading to a great bronze door. Fergus was astonished by this discovery but he never faltered. He climbed the stairs and before he reached the door it was thrown open and a tall young man invited him inside. He was taller than King Conor himself and his hair flowed down to his purple cape. Fergus did not realise that this was Lugh of the Long Arm, god of the harvest, defeater of Balor of the Evil Eye.

A beautiful, fair-haired girl stepped out from behind Lugh. It was Dechtera; the druid's long lost daughter! She welcomed Fergus warmly and asked him for news of the court and tidings of her father. She asked Fergus to tell her father that Lugh himself had lured her to Tír na nÓg, the Land of Faery and to bring word to her father that she was very happy but could never return.

Fergus was treated with great hospitality in the marble palace that night. Beautiful maidens served the finest food and drink to him. The night passed quickly as he was entertained with music and sweet singing.

In the morning, Fergus took his leave and returned to the other warriors who were just rising and stretching. On a blanket, by the river, they discovered a sleeping baby boy. Dechtera had lured them to Lugh's fairy palace to ensure that her son would be raised at King Conor's court, amongst her own people.

When the king and his men returned to court, the old druid rejoiced over his new found grandson. He was delighted with the news of his daughter and he was honoured that the great Lugh had chosen her. Ever after, Cathbad told with great pride, the story of how his grandson had returned from Tír na nÓg.

Dechtera's sister and her husband Sualdam agreed to raise the baby as their foster-child. They called him Setanta, and everyone knew he was destined for great deeds.

How Cúchulainn earned his name

At that time, the warrior skills were taught to the children at King Conor's court. In addition to learning how to handle a sword and shield, they had to learn the stories of their ancestors and the skills of the game of hurling.

Young Setanta began his warrior training when he was seven years old. He became so skilled at hurling that before long, he could take on an entire team and defeat them all on his own. News of this reached the king, who was a great admirer of the sport.

One day, on his way to the house of his blacksmith, King Conor stopped his chariot to watch Setanta play a hurling game. The youngster could raise the ball with his hurley stick and hit a puck over the bar from far out in mid-field. When the hurlers took a break, the king called out to Setanta: 'Fine playing, my lad. I am impressed. I am on my way to Cullen's house for dinner, I would like you to join me.'

'Your Majesty, I would be glad to join you, but I would first of all like to finish this game.'

'I understand, my boy, finish your game, then follow the tracks of my chariot through the woods and you will come to the blacksmith's house.'

The king rode away at full speed and soon arrived at Cullen's house.

Cullen's skill as a smith was renowned. He made the weapons for the Red Branch warriors and often entertained the king at his home. He gave the king a warm welcome and asked if he was ready to eat.

'Indeed I am, Cullen,' said the king, forgetting about his invitation to the boy, 'and I have brought a hearty appetite with me.'

'Right enough,' said Cullen. 'My family is settled in the dining-hall. The pig is roasted and awaits our carving. Let me first lock up the gates and release my hound to guard the house.'

Cullen owned a large, Irish wolfhound, a faithful watchdog. Having released the dog, he returned to the dining-room and they began their meal.

Meanwhile, young Setanta finished his game of hurling, soundly defeating the other team. He set off through the woods following the tracks of the king's chariot. He brought his hurley stick and leather ball with him and as he walked along he

tossed the ball in the air, then ran ahead and caught it before it hit the ground. In this way, he soon reached the walls of Cullen's house but he found that the gates were locked and the only way inside was to jump over the wall. This he did, but when he landed down on the other side, the hound came rushing at him with his mouth open and his teeth bared.

Setanta had to think quickly to save himself. An idea flashed in his mind and he tossed the ball in the air and hit it a mighty blow with the hurley stick. The ball hit the hound between the eyes and he fell, dead to the ground.

When King Conor heard the commotion, he remembered that he had invited Setanta to join them for dinner. He came rushing from the house expecting to find the boy dead, or at least badly injured. He was delighted to find him unharmed.

Cullen followed the king outside and was horrified to find that his hound was dead.

'Don't be angry,' said Setanta, 'I had no other choice to save myself. But if you give me a pup belonging to this hound, I will train it to be just as good a watch-dog as its father. In the meantime, Cullen, I will act as a watch-dog for you and will guard your home.'

'Well spoken, young man,' said the king. 'From this time on your name shall be changed to Cú-chulainn, meaning the Hound of Cullen. All will know that this is the name of a great warrior.'

Cúchulainn receives a warrior's weapons

Cúchulainn spent many years in warrior training at King Conor's court. One day, he heard Cathbad, the druid, say that a youth who received the weapons of a man on that day would be one of Ireland's greatest warriors but his life would be short and dangerous.

Instantly, Cúchulainn went before the king and demanded the weapons of manhood. The king smiled down at the young lad, who, although strong and sturdily built, was not very tall. Nevertheless, Conor handed two full-sized spears to the boy. Cúchulainn broke them in half as if they were twigs. The king sent for two more spears, but Cúchulainn broke these just as easily and went on breaking spears until finally the king sent for his own sword and spear. The boy could not break them.

With the king's own weapons at his side, Cúchulainn then climbed into Conor's chariot and told the charioteer that he was in search of deeds of valour. 'Can you help me to prove my warrior skills?' he asked the charioteer.

The charioteer drove Cúchulainn to the top of

highest hill, from where he could see over all the countryside. The charioteer pointed out the forts of all the local chieftains, and the last one he showed Cúchulainn belonged to the three fierce sons of Nechtan the Mighty. 'It is said that those three warriors have killed more men than there are alive in Ulster,' said the charioteer.

'I will challenge them, this very day,' said Cúchulainn, jumping into the chariot.

'It would be a foolish thing for you, a young lad, to challenge these fierce men,' replied the charioteer.

'Take me there now!' ordered Cúchulainn.

The charioteer knew it was useless to argue with the boy and did as Cúchulainn requested.

They stopped in front of the fort and Cúchulainn dismounted. Immediately, the door was thrown open and the eldest brother, Foill, came rushing outside. When he saw the young lad, he shrugged his shoulders and turned around to go back inside. He was about to close the door when Cúchulainn challenged him to combat and told him to get his weapons.

When Foill returned, ready to fight, Cúchulainn put a small stone into his sling and threw it at

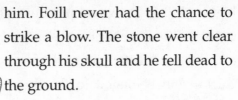him. Foill never had the chance to strike a blow. The stone went clear through his skull and he fell dead to the ground.

Then the other two brothers came running out of the fort and quick as a flash, Cúchulainn dealt them the same deadly blows. Then he cut the heads from the three sons of Nechtan and tied them to the rim of his chariot.

As Cúchulainn was making his way back to Eamhain Macha, he came upon a herd of deer, led by a big, handsome stag. The deer ran into the woods as the chariot approached and Cúchulainn asked the charioteer, 'do you think the men at court would prefer to have this stag brought back to them dead, or alive?'

The charioteer was astonished by the question.

'Why, they would prefer to see you return with a live one, it would surprise them more. No man has ever returned with a live deer although each man has brought back one that he killed in the hunt. I do not think it is possible for you, just a young lad, to catch one alive.'

'It is possible,' answered Cúchulainn.

Then asking his charioteer to urge the horses on to their greatest speed, they gave chase to the herd of deer. Gradually, they closed the gap between themselves and the deer, as the king's own horses were the swiftest in the land. They began to pass the deer and when they were level with the great stag's head, Cúchulainn called out to him. His voice was mysterious and the charioteer did not understand the words. But the stag turned his head and looked at the boy. Cúchulainn's gaze was so deep and penetrating that the stag stopped running and allowed Cúchulainn to leap onto his back. Holding onto the stag's antlers, Cúchulainn remained seated on the stag's back on their journey homeward.

When they were still a distance from Eamhain Macha, Cúchulainn saw a flock of geese flying overhead. Quickly he pulled out his sling and brought down sixteen geese, still alive. These he also tied to the rim of the chariot. Then he proudly went back to the court.

News of his accomplishments preceded him

and a crowd collected to watch his triumphant return. A cheer greeted Cúchulainn as he arrived at Eamhain Macha, riding the wild stag. Behind him came his chariot with the three heads strapped to it and the flock of geese flying overhead.

Cúchulainn in the Land of Shadows

Soon, Cúchulainn was the talk of the king's court, not only for his warrior skills but because he was growing up and becoming a handsome young man. Time came for him to choose a wife and Cúchulainn had eyes for only one girl in the land.

He wanted Emer, the fair-haired daughter of Fergal Monach, an Ulster chieftain. Cúchulainn had seen Emer at court and had instantly fallen in love with her. He thought her the fairest, the most beautiful girl who ever lived. One day, he decided that it was time to seek her hand in marriage and so he set out in his chariot for the fort of Emer's father.

Emer herself greeted Cúchulainn at the door of her father's fort. She smiled at her young suitor but when he asked her to marry him, she replied, 'Cúchulainn, my father plans for me to marry a king, he wants me to bring wealth to the family.'

She saw the look of disappointment appear on Cúchulainn's face and she continued, 'but if you were a champion warrior, I myself would choose you as a husband.'

There and then, Cúchulainn decided to become

the champion of Ireland and win the hand of Emer.

At that time, women often taught warriors and the most famous teacher of all was a woman named Scatha who lived in the Land of Shadows. She was famous throughout the Celtic world yet few knew the way to the Land of Shadows.

Having searched throughout Ireland for many days, Cúchulainn finally arrived on the rocky coast of the north-east. There, he met an old man who told him he would need to sail to Scatha's island, way off to the north. He peered at the strong young man, 'Take my boat and my blessing and be on your way. You have a dangerous journey ahead.'

Cúchulainn thanked the old man and pushed the boat out into the sea. The waves were high and rough and water splashed over the sides, but Cúchulainn set the boat towards the north-east and did not look back. All day and night the winds blew strong. At dawn on the following morning, cold and hungry, he reached Alba, his destination. He picked the small boat off the water and placed it safely on some flat rocks. Then he set out to find Scatha.

All through that rocky countryside he journeyed, asking everyone he met how to reach the

Land of Shadows. But none could show him the way. This country was wilder than Cúchulainn had ever seen before. Towards the day's end, when he was growing weary from travel, he rounded a bend by the sea and came upon a group of boys playing a game of hurling in a wide, open field high up on the side of a cliff. Bordering one side of the field was a drop from the cliff to the surging sea below. On the other side of this gorge, the land jutted forward again and led to a fort set up on a hill.

The boys stopped playing and crowded around Cúchulainn, asking him who he was and his reason for being there. 'I am a warrior of King Conor's Red Branch of Ulster and I seek Scatha, for I have heard that she is the greatest trainer of warriors.'

Cúchulainn then learned that each of these boys was in the training of Scatha.

'But where is she?' asked Cúchulainn.

The boys pointed across the gorge to the fort on the hill. 'That is Scatha's fort,' said one of the lads. 'This is our training ground and our camp is here. She comes to teach us each day across the Bridge of Leaps. It is that narrow plank over there.' The boy pointed to a thin plank suspended from cliff to cliff. 'No one but Scatha can cross that bridge,' continued

24

the boy, 'for if you step on one end, the middle rises up and flings you back, and if you try to jump onto it, it is so slippery that you will surely fall down onto the jagged rocks below. Come, have dinner and rest with us. Scatha will come to us tomorrow.'

'But that bridge is there and ready to be crossed,' said Cúchulainn, 'and I do not care to wait another day to meet Scatha.'

'Scatha does not agree to train all who come to find her,' continued the boy. 'There are many she has turned away. But her chosen champions are taught how to cross the Bridge of Leaps but only at the end of their training. She also teaches these warriors how to use the Ga Bolga, the deadly body spear thrown with the foot.'

Cúchulainn agreed to rest and eat dinner with the other young warriors. But while they were still eating, he left the table and headed for the Bridge of Leaps. When he reached it, he looked back and saw that all the boys were watching him. He turned and gave a running jump at the bridge. He landed near the middle of the plank and was tossed back. He heard the cheers from below and tried again. Again and again he was tossed back but on his fourth try he landed right in the centre of the bridge and sprang forward onto the other side. He walked on up the cliff to the fort where Scatha was waiting for him at the door.

The woman smiled at Cúchulainn and told him that he need search no further. 'Your fame proceeds you, Cúchulainn,' she said. 'I have heard of how you earned your name. I will accept you as my student and teach you warrior skills. You will be a good match for Ferdia, the boy you spoke with over there in the camp. He, too, is from Ireland where his father is a chieftain in Connacht.'

Cúchulainn was glad to learn that the boy was Irish also. He had liked him from the moment they first met. Ferdia was a dark-haired youth, no taller than Cúchulainn, with broad, strong shoulders. From that time onward, they became friends and were inseparable while in training in the Land of Shadows. They became so skilled that often they fought by Scatha's side in the wars amongst the tribes of Alba and no one could defeat the three of them when they fought together.

At the end of a year and a day, Scatha called the two young warriors to her fort. 'The time has come for you to return to your homeland. I am sad to see you go, but I have no more to teach you.'

She took Cúchulainn aside and taught him to use the Ga Bolga, or body spear. Then she gave him her own, for he was the first warrior she thought worthy to use it. This spear was thrown with the foot and when it entered a warrior's body it filled every limb with its barbs. Cúchulainn promised to use it wisely and only as a last resort in battle.

Ferdia and Cúchulainn travelled homeward together across the Irish Sea, but once they reached land, Ferdia took his leave of Cúchulainn and headed south into Leinster. He told Cúchulainn that he had no wish to remain even for a day in Ulster as his queen in Connacht was the sworn enemy of King Conor. They parted sadly, promising friendship as long as they lived.

Cúchulainn becomes Champion of Ireland

King Conor and his court were celebrating the feast of Samhain on the night when Cúchulainn returned from the Land of Shadows. The great hall was crowded and noisy; warriors were feasting and laughing; some were dancing jigs while musicians played over in the corner.

King Conor sat on his throne at one end of the great hall and appeared to be arguing with two warriors who stood before him. The old druid, Cathbad, sat by the king's side and listened to all that was being said.

Suddenly, he glanced toward the door and saw Cúchulainn standing there, quietly observing the activities of the room. Cathbad rose and called out, 'My child, you have come back to us. Look, everyone, Cúchulainn has returned.'

A huge crowd, all eager to hear of his adventures across the sea, quickly surrounded Cúchulainn. After a brief discussion with his friends of the Red Branch, Cúchulainn calmly and quietly approached the king's throne.

'Welcome home, Cúchulainn,' King Conor smiled at the lad, thinking how manly he now looked. No longer a boy, still small in stature, but quite grown up.

'Your Highness, I hear talk of a contest. May I be allowed to join in?'

The king laughed aloud and turned to his druid, 'Cathbad, my friend, what a dilemma! Each of these warriors says he deserves to be called the champion of Ireland and now your grandson asks to participate in the contest. But what contest! I know not how to choose. Can you, with your infinite wisdom, devise such a contest?'

A smile spread across the old druid's wizened face. 'Yes, Your Majesty. This I can do. I shall return shortly. Warriors prepare your swords.'

He arose and walked from the hall, trailing his long, dark red cloak behind him.

The warriors' faces expressed their puzzlement. They took their swords from their scabbards strapped to their sides. They ran their fingers lightly down the blades. All but Cúchulainn appeared nervous. The king smiled comfortably now, the problem had been taken care of – as far as he was concerned.

Moments later, the door was flung open by two scuttling servants and a huge, giant of a man entered, wearing a short red cloak. His eyes bulged forth as he looked fiercely at the warriors. His massive head with his thick grey hair sat on his broad, shoulders. His legs were like tree trunks and his feet like two enormous boulders. He held a long thin sword with both hands as he slowly approached the astonished warriors.

King Conor was the only person with a smile on his face, as he realised that this was Cathbad, whose druidic powers allowed him to change his shape.

The giant towered above the warriors. 'I offer you a challenge,' his voice boomed. 'Each of you in turn may fight me and attempt to cut my head off, if you will then allow me to retaliate.'

The warriors smiled, one even snickered, thinking that a headless giant would be no trouble to them.

They accepted the challenge and the first warrior to step forward was Laoighre, son of a Connacht chieftain. He fought bravely against the giant and finally, with one mighty stroke, he sliced the giant's head right off his huge shoulders. Blood spurted from the neck, but the giant ignored the cries of the crowd and merely bent down, picked up his head, and replaced it on his shoulders. Then, holding his sword up in the air, he approached Laoighre. Terrified, the young warrior dropped his sword and fled from the great hall.

The crowd roared with laughter and another warrior, Conall Cearnach, stepped forward slowly and without enthusiasm. Yet he also fought bravely against the giant and managed to cut off the giant's head. Once again, the giant replaced his head and loomed over the warrior, his sword glinting in the candle-light. Conall Cearnach let a yelp out of him and ran for his life.

Cúchulainn stepped forward to the cheers of the crowd. All knew of this young man's bravery when, as a boy, he had earned his name by killing the ferocious hound of Cullen. The giant smiled down at Cúchulainn and raised his sword. The fight between them was long and fierce. Finally, Cúchulainn came in low and swiped upward at the giant's neck. The head rolled to the floor with a dull thud. The giant slowly picked it up and replaced it on his shoulders. As he turned back to Cúchulainn, the young man dropped his sword and bent his head toward the giant offering him the chance to retaliate.

Instead, the giant immediately transformed into his true form, that of Cathbad the druid, the red cloak now, once again, trailing on the floor. Beaming at the audience, he grasped Cúchulainn's hand and raised it aloft, shouting out, 'Your Majesty, we have found the true champion of Ireland! Young Cúchulainn was the only warrior who did not run away, the only warrior who was brave enough to keep his word and allow me to retaliate.'

Thunderous applause erupted in the hall. The crowd rose to its feet, they slammed the wooden tables with fists and spoons. Cúchulainn was picked up, off the ground, and placed on the shoulders of two strong men. They carried him up the great hall and placed him on the ground before the king. Conor smiled at the slight stature of Ireland's champion. Cúchulainn was not shy to return the smile. His tossed hair lay in thick curls on his shoulders.

'Cúchulainn, you have earned yourself the leadership of my Red Branch warriors. There is not a man in the province who would dispute it. Come, let us celebrate. Musicians, music!' The king placed Cúchulainn beside him and ordered food and drink to be brought for the champion.

As soon as he was able, Cúchulainn took his leave of the king and, finding Laeg, his charioteer waiting outside, he asked him to quickly bring his chariot to the door. Minutes later, Cúchulainn clutched the reins and urged Macha, his beautiful grey mare to gallop at full speed. They pulled up sharply at the home of Emer and her father.

Before Cúchulainn could dismount, the great door was flung open and Emer's father came striding over the path closely followed by Emer who was trying to keep up with her father. Cúchulainn braced himself, expecting opposition from the man, but as he drew closer, a smile spread across the older man's face and he reached his hand out to grasp Cúchulainn's hand and shake it soundly.

'My boy, we have heard, we have heard of the great honour that the king has bestowed upon you. News of your bravery cannot be concealed. Let us go inside. My daughter has expressed a wish to see you.' Then turning about with a great sweep of his cloak, he led them back inside.

Much bustling about followed, as he shouted at servants to bring food and drink, and set the fire ablaze. Finally they sat down to a meal and Cúchulainn realised that this man would accept him as a husband for his daughter. He gazed across the table at Emer, her red hair shining in the firelight and her face aglow with happiness. Cúchulainn knew that he had found his match in this woman, she would be strong and able for him in every way.

A wedding feast took place at the court at Eamhain Macha and the like of it was never seen before! Fergal decided that if his daughter would not marry a king, he would instead provide her with the most royal of weddings!

Afterwards, Cúchulainn and Emer went to live in nearby Dún Dealgan and settled down happily to their lives together.

Cúchulainn in the Land of Faery

A short time after the great wedding, the men at Eamhain Macha arranged to go on a deer hunt. Venison meat was in high demand at court and it was time to replenish the supplies. Cúchulainn went along with the other warriors. They left at daybreak and shortly afterwards Cúchulainn spied, in a thicket, a lone deer standing quietly. He raised his spear and softly rushed forward, but the deer ran off and led Cúchulainn onto an open plain, then down into a valley that was bare of trees or bushes. Cúchulainn thought that he had the deer trapped and prepared to fling his spear. But right before his eyes, the deer vanished! There was no place in that glen where the deer could have hidden, he had just disappeared!

Shocked by this strange occurrence and suddenly overcome by a strange feeling of weakness, Cúchulainn sat down to rest on the grass. He became so weak that he could not stand up again, nor even call for help.

Hours later, the Red Branch warriors found him huddled on the ground, pale and unable to walk. They felt an easiness in that valley and wondered if some magical force was the cause of Cúchulainn's condition. As quickly as possible, the warriors wrapped Cúchulainn in their cloaks and carried him home to Emer. She was shocked when she saw his condition and sent the warriors onward to Eamhain Macha, asking them to return with Cathbad, the druid.

The old druid arrived with his bag of potions, but taking one look at Cúchulainn's tired, pale face he gave a deep sigh. 'Out of Faeryland did you come to us long ago, my son, and the people of that land retain strong ties with you. I fear that this is their work. We have no way of knowing why they have chosen to put you in this state.'

Cathbad tried several of his most powerful spells and potions, but nothing worked. Cúchulainn lay for seven days in his weak state. Emer was beside herself with grief, thinking he might die. She never left his side, catching quick naps in a chair by his bedside.

On the seventh night, she awoke from a nap to see her husband sit bolt upright in bed and call out in his sleep, 'no, do not ask me to return there.' Then Cúchulainn lay back down on his pillow and opened his eyes.

For the first time in seven days, he recognised her and a faint smile crossed his face at the sight of her. 'I have had a strange dream,' he said, 'a man wearing a green silk cloak appeared to me and told me that my cure lies in the same glen where the sickness came upon me. He said I must return there immediately. Then he walked away from my bed and as he did, I noticed that he had a beautiful stag embroidered on the back of his cloak.'

Cúchulainn saw Emer's worried face and hurriedly said, 'I must go back there. It is my only hope of recovering my strength.'

'I will go with you,' said Emer.

'No, I was told to come alone,' said Cúchulainn.

Nothing Emer could say would persuade her husband not to go. He summoned Laeg, his faithful charioteer, and asked him to carry him to the chariot and to bring him to the magic glen. Then Cúchulainn asked Laeg to leave him there alone. The charioteer had just driven away out of sight when a fairy woman appeared wearing a long red cloak.

'Who are you?' asked Cúchulainn.

'I am a messenger from Fann, a queen of Tír na nÓg, the Land of Faery,' replied the stranger. 'Fann has sent me to ask you to come to Faeryland to help her defeat three evil kings who are attacking her country.'

'Look at me!' exclaimed Cúchulainn, 'I am in no condition to help anyone, not even myself. Why does Fann not ask for aid from her husband, Manann Mac Lir, the king of the sea?'

'They have quarrelled and he has left her. You must come to help her. You will find that your strength will return once you promise to visit Fann in Tír na nÓg.'

Cúchulainn mulled this idea over in his head.

'Well?' queried the messenger, 'will you come to help Fann?'

'I will come on one condition,' replied Cúchulainn. 'Let my charioteer, Laeg, go there before me and come back to tell me what it is like.'

'It shall be so,' said the messenger. With a great sweep of her long cloak, she turned around and disappeared!

Cúchulainn instantly felt his strength returning to him. He felt the blood surging through his veins and he sprang to his feet. He ran after Laeg and overtook the chariot long before it reached Eamhain Macha. He told Laeg to return at once to the enchanted glen. 'Someone will meet you there and bring you to Tír na nÓg. 'I want you to go to Faeryland to see what it is like.'

Then Cúchulainn hurried home to Emer. She was delighted to find his health restored to him, but was not happy when he told her of his decision to go to the aid of the queen of Faeryland.

'Do not leave me,' she pleaded, 'I am afraid that some evil magic will prevent you from returning to me.'

'Emer, my love,' replied Cúchulainn, 'I have given my word and will never break it. But let us not discuss the matter until Laeg comes back.'

When Laeg returned from the Land of Faery, he sang its praises. 'It is the most beautiful place I have ever visited.'

'What of its queen, Fann, what is she like?' asked Cúchulainn.

'She is tall and fair and very beautiful, perhaps the most beautiful woman I have ever seen,' said Laeg. Then he quickly added, 'except for Emer.'

'Did she send any message for me?' asked Cúchulainn.

'She did,' replied Laeg, 'she asked me to remind you of your promise to her.'

Cúchulainn was deeply troubled. He had no wish to go to the Land of Faery. He knew that he had come from there as a baby and was afraid that if he now returned, he might be unable to leave again. But he could not break his promise to Fann.

After much thought, he went to Emer and told her that he must go to help Fann.

'I am afraid that you will forget me and never come back,' she said.

'That could never happen, Emer,' he laughed, 'I love you more than my own life. I will return to you very soon.'

'Just to be certain,' said Emer, 'I am putting a *geas* on you to promise to come back home in one month.'

'You do not need to put that spell on me, I plan to be back in a few days,' joked Cúchulainn.

When Cúchulainn arrived in Tír na nÓg, he found it to be just as beautiful as Laeg had described. He was instantly brought to the magnificent court of the queen and was astounded by her beauty. When Fann looked at Cúchulainn, her green eyes flashed a look of longing at him and he fell in love with her on the spot.

'I am glad that you are well and strong again,' she said to him. 'Now, you will be able to defeat my enemies.' Fann then told Cúchulainn that three giants who ruled the neighbouring land tormented her and her people. They were descendants of Fomorian giants and their kind had ruled that land for centuries. There had been peace between them since Lugh had defeated Balor of the Evil Eye, long ago, but now the land of the giants was ruled by three evil brothers who were nothing but bullies.

'They have not an ounce of intelligence between them, but they believe that they are powerful because of their size. They have crushed several of our people for no reason other than that they were walking close to the border between the two lands. We have no warriors here with skills to compare with yours. Do this for me and I will reward you well.'

'I need no reward at all. I want only to return home safely.'

Cúchulainn picked up his weapons and set out for the land of the giants. He arrived at the border and saw that there were giant sentries on guard. Cúchulainn called out to one of them and demanded to be brought before the kings. 'I have important business with your kings,' he said. The man agreed to show him the way. Cúchulainn walked beside the sentry, but only reached up to the giant's shoulder.

While they were walking, Cúchulainn said to the giant, 'I have heard much grumbling about the rulers of this land.' Cúchulainn paused and glanced at the giant, wondering if he would say something.

'I'm not surprised,' said the giant heatedly. 'There's nothing but complaints to be heard, these days. They don't care about anybody, but themselves. And they really shouldn't be ruling the country at all. The leadership belongs to the son who most deserves to rule. Those three don't know how to rule a land. But they stole the throne from the fourth brother who should rightly be our king.' The giant stopped talking and took a deep breath.

They soon arrived at the fort of the giants. It was a huge wooden building, set into the hillside. The sentry went inside and a few seconds later, the great door was thrown open and one of the kings came out. His huge face was red with anger, 'I'm going to kill the little man!' he roared.

He carried a sword in his hand and his hair was

tied back from his face but was so long that it reached almost to the ground. He lunged forward at Cúchulainn with his sword but Cúchulainn nimbly stepped to the giant's side. He reached up and cut the giant's hair ribbon, setting his hair free. Immediately, the giant's hair fell over his face and all the way down to his ankles. His legs became entangled in it and he fell to the ground. Quick as lightning, Cúchulainn cut off his head.

Instantly, another giant appeared at the door. Cúchulainn cringed. This giant's breath was so foul that when he walked near the trees, all the leaves fell to the ground.

Cúchulainn leaped forward and swiped with his axe at the giant's ankles. The giant jumped in the air to avoid the axe and turned himself around. He caught a whiff of his own breath and it sent him reeling backward. Cúchulainn was ready and catching him off guard, he cut the giant's head from his body. Then he placed both heads just outside the door of the giant's fort.

The third king came rushing out of the fort and immediately fell over the two huge heads on the ground. As soon as he hit the ground, Cúchulainn cut his head from his shoulders. He then tied all three heads together and wondered how he would carry them back to Fann.

Suddenly he heard a cheer behind him and turning around, he saw another giant approaching. This giant was smiling and all the people of the kingdom were cheering. He walked right up to Cúchulainn 'thank you, for saving our land from my brothers,' he said. 'They have kept me imprisoned for many years and my people have been troubled. I thank you for rescuing us.'

He gave a low bow, which Cúchulainn returned.

The giant then arranged for two other giants to carry the heads back to the land of Faery and deliver them to Fann. Cúchulainn also brought a message from the new king that peace would be restored between the lands.

Fann was very happy to receive the news and to find Cúchulainn unharmed. 'My reward to you,' she said, 'is that you will live here happily evermore and not remember your former life.'

So Cúchulainn stayed in the Land of Faery. The weeks passed and he was very happy, having forgotten all about his love for Emer.

Just before the month was up, the *geas* began to

take hold of Cúchulainn and he remembered that he had to return to Emer. He told Fann that he had to leave her but he promised to meet her again and so she agreed to let him go.

Emer was delighted when she saw Cúchulainn return home. She ran to meet him and hugged him to her. 'Oh, I was so afraid that you would not return,' she whispered to him. Then she looked into his eyes and she sensed that something was wrong. 'You do not love me anymore,' she said, 'you have changed.'

'Of course I have not!' protested Cúchulainn

But Emer knew that he had not the same strong love for her that he used to have. She watched him closely, suspecting that he was under a spell.

When Cúchulainn went to meet Fann at the seashore, Emer followed with seven of her maidens. Each of the women carried a long, sharp knife! Emer had decided that she was going to do whatever was necessary to win back the love of Cúchulainn, even if this meant killing her rival.

When Fann appeared, Cúchulainn hugged her to him. Suddenly, the women rushed out from behind a great yew tree, brandishing their knives.

'Kill that woman,' shouted Emer as they advanced toward Fann.

Fann screamed and clung to Cúchulainn. Cúchulainn stood in front of her to protect her. He faced the women: 'Why are you doing this?' he asked Emer.

'Because she has stolen you from me,' she replied

'But I love her,' Cúchulainn pleaded.

'You loved me once more than your own life. You told me so and I saw the truth in your eyes. She has placed you under a spell and has stolen your love away from me,' sobbed Emer.

'But I still love you, Emer,' said Cúchulainn.

Fann was crying softly behind Cúchulainn but now she began to wail out loud. She knew that she could never take Cúchulainn away from Emer, their love was more powerful than her magic.

Her husband, Manann Mac Lir, heard her sorrowful wails and appeared by her side. He placed his arm around her. 'Will you come away with me?' he asked her softly, 'I am sorry that we quarrelled. You must know that I love you very much.'

Fann nodded her head and, speechless, she buried her face in his shoulder. Then the Lord of the Sea wrapped his cloak around Fann and they both disappeared.

Cúchulainn was shocked when he realised that Fann had left him. Her spell was still on him and he felt great love for her. He sat down on the ground, unable to decide what to do next.

Emer sent her maidens on ahead to Eamhain Macha with a message for the druid. She asked him to prepare a potion for Cúchulainn that would cure him of this sickness. Then she put her arm around her husband and led him homeward. Old Cathbad was waiting for them when they arrived, with a reassuring smile on his face. He handed Cúchulainn a goblet filled with a green liquid. He had also prepared one for Emer. 'But I'm not under any spell!' she protested.

'My child,' said old Cathbad. 'You have been through an ordeal that would best be erased from your memory. Drink now with your husband.'

So Cúchulainn and Emer both drank the potion and instantly they forgot all about Fann and her mischief. From that time onward, Cúchulainn and Emer were happy in their lives together and nothing ever threatened their love for each other again.

The Cattle Raid of Cooley

Queen Maeve's throne was set up on a pedestal at one end of the great hall. It was her favourite seat in the fort. Just beside the window, she could look out over her vast kingdom of Connacht.

Her pet raven perched on her shoulder, his beady little eyes flashing about the room. The queen gave a deep sigh and drummed her finger on the arm of the bejewelled throne.

The sunlight came through the window and Maeve's gaze fell on the white bull in the meadow down below. He was a brawny, white-horned bull and as she watched, he raised his head up proudly and trotted to the far end of the green meadow.

The queen turned from the window and tossed her long golden hair over her shoulder.

Her raven flew about the hall, then returned and sat again on her shoulder just as King Ailell entered the room. He was a short, pale-faced man with drooping shoulders. Maeve eyed him haughtily and remained on her pedestal, wondering as she watched his approach why she had allowed her father to convince her to marry this oaf. True, he had wealth but so had she. He had land but so had she and would inherit more from her father, the high king, who lived at Tara. Her father had thought it a golden opportunity to ally with Connacht by marrying his daughter to the king of that province. But there was no love between Maeve and Ailell.

Just two days earlier, Maeve had begun to taunt her husband that she in fact had greater wealth that he. Ailell immediately rose to the bait and began to recite all of his possessions in a long list. Maeve retaliated and matched his list with her own.

All evening long they continued and long into the night, matching their gold and jewels, the spears and swords of their warriors, their chariots and horses, their flocks of sheep and acres of land. When they found that they were equal in every way they fell asleep, exhausted.

Maeve had arranged a fox hunt for the next morning, but, as the queen sat astride her grey stallion and was about to gallop after her hounds, her husband came running from the fort and detained her. Angrily, she pulled up her horse and glared down at Ailell: 'What is so important that you must tell me now?' she asked through clenched teeth.

'I have just remembered Finnbennach, my fine white-horned bull,' Ailell smiled, gesturing with his arm toward the meadow. 'You do not have his equal in your herd.'

Maeve's lips compressed into a thin line and, speechless, she glared down at her husband. Then digging her heels into the sides of her horse, she galloped out of the court-yard without another word.

Now, two days later, she strained to hide her rage as her husband shuffled up the great hall in the slippers he wore day and night! She knew that the smirk on his face was due to the fact that he thought he had won the argument and defeated her. He could now boast of having greater possessions than she, for she did not have a bull to equal his. Maeve would not admit that she had been defeated. 'Never!' she thought, 'I'll never let him get the better of me!' Turning her back on her husband, she left the room by a small door near her throne. Her raven flew out the window.

Furious, Maeve sent for messengers to come to her room. Mac Roth, her steward, led them in. The queen immediately turned to him with questions. 'I need a bull the equal of my husband's white-horned bull. Is there such a bull to be found any-where in Ireland?'

'There is indeed, Your Highness. It is called the Brown Bull of Cooley and it belongs to Dara Mac Fiachna, a farmer who lives in Ulster. It is said to be the noblest bull in all of Ireland.'

Maeve now longed for this bull more than any-thing else in the world. 'Go,' she told the messen-gers. 'Seek out Dara Mac Fiachna and tell him that Queen Maeve of Connacht would like the loan of his bull for a year. In return, I will give him a piece of land here in Connacht as big as what he owns in Ulster. He shall also have 50 heifers and my honour and esteem as long as he lives.'

The messengers set out for Ulster with many gifts and arrived, late in the evening, at Dara's house. They presented their gifts and Dara was delighted with the offer. He agreed to the bargain and sent for food and wine to be brought for the messengers.

As they were tired and hungry, the messengers ate and drank their fill. But as more and stronger wine was sent for, their tongues were loosened and they became boastful.

One young fellow said, 'it is well for Dara Mac

Fiachna that he has agreed to grant Maeve this wish, for if he had refused, she herself would have taken the bull by force.'

Quickly, the news reached Dara and in a rage, he threw the messengers out of his home, calling after them: 'Tell your queen that she will never get her hands on my bull. Ulster will fight to keep what is ours.'

A cold, wet dawn was breaking when the messengers arrived home. When Maeve heard the news, she flew into a great rage and ordered Mac Roth to throw the messengers in the dungeon. She paced the floor, her servants hovering nearby with a candle. Back and forth she paced, then paused at the window and gazed out into the darkness outside. It was coming close to Samhain and anything was possible. The moon shone brightly down on the meadow and Maeve glimpsed a white hoof in flight.

The next morning, Maeve sent for Fergus Mac Roy, one of her finest warriors. Fergus was from Ulster and had come over to Maeve's side because of a falling out with King Conor. Maeve sought information from Fergus. Although Fergus now belonged to Maeve's army, he did not trust this queen.

'Tell me Fergus,' she began, 'what do you know of the Brown Bull of Cooley?'

Fergus was surprised by this question, and wondered how the bull could interest Maeve.

'That bull belongs to Dara Mac Fiachna, in the province of Ulster. It is said that only King Ailell's bull, Finnbennach of the White Horns, is his equal. They are the strongest, broadest bulls in the land and many believe that it is out of Faeryland that they came. Your Majesty should ask her storytellers if she would like to know more.'

Fergus bowed to Maeve.

'Indeed I can do that, Fergus,' laughed Maeve, 'but I have another question for you. We have heard of the curse that was put on the men of Ulster and know that it comes upon the warriors at the outset of winter. Will we find that Ulster is un-defended if we attack? For I plan to invade Ulster and bring back this Brown Bull of Cooley.'

Fergus was not forthcoming with information about the Brown Bull or about the warrior spell, but Maeve understood that he still retained his ties with Ulster. She called for Fedelma, her storyteller and prophetess and asked her for the full story of Ulster and Fergus Mac Roy.

Maeve sent for Ailell and ordered the fires to be set ablaze in the great hall. She was looking forward to hearing this story. Fedelma was highly skilled in the art of storytelling and she also had the power to foretell the future.

The storyteller settled herself in the corner and when the royal couple were ready she began to tell her story of Ulster.

'Long ago, Fachtna, the giant, was king of Ulster and Nessa was his queen. They had one child, a boy named Conor. When Fachtna died, Fergus Mac Roy, his half-brother, became king for Conor was still a youth. Now Nessa was still a beautiful woman and Fergus fell in love with her and asked her to be his wife. Nessa agreed on one condition. "Let my son Conor rule Ulster just for one year so that his children and his children's children can say that they are descended from kings."

'Fergus was an easy-going man, more suited to outdoor life rather than attending to the affairs of state. He wanted to please Nessa so he agreed to her bargain.

'So Conor became king and during that year, Nessa coached her son in all the affairs of state. She gave him gold to spend on feasting the nobles at court and more gold to give to his people to win their favour. She succeeded in guiding him to rule the province wisely and everyone was content with his rule and said there never was a wiser king or one who made Ulster so prosperous.

'When the time came for Fergus to take back the throne, the nobles and the people banded together to keep Conor as their king. They said that Fergus must not have cared much for the throne in the first place, if he was willing to give it up for a woman!

'For a time, Fergus was content to allow Conor to remain as king. Fergus was a fine warrior, but he had the heart of a poet, not a ruler, and for many years he enjoyed living at the court.

'But Conor was a vain king and with his mother's guidance, he became wealthy and powerful.

'It happened, at that time, that the goddess Macha came out of Faeryland and fell in love with an Ulster farmer. He took her for his wife and she happily helped him with work on the farm. At Samhain time, her husband went to the annual festival at court, but his wife preferred to remain at home. She asked him to keep her identity a secret, but after a few drinks in the company of warriors, he could not stop himself from boasting of his wife, after all, she had the beauty of a goddess and wondrous magical powers.

'"She even has the swiftness of a deer," he said, "she could outrun Conor's swiftest steed."

'It was not long before news reached Conor of this woman's attributes. Jealous and envious by nature, he could not bear to think that she could outshine him. He thought to show her up in public, not realising that she was a goddess. He ordered the farmer to go home and return with his wife to race against the royal racehorses.

'The farmer immediately regretted his boasts and told the king that his wife was very close to giving birth. He pleaded with the king to accept his apology for his boasting, but Conor scoffed at him and insisted that the contest take place.

'Macha, although heavy with child, agreed to the bargain, knowing that if she refused, her husband would be killed for making idle boasts. She defeated the steeds in a foot race, but collapsed at the finish line. "I shall leave this land behind," she called out, "but before I leave, I put a curse on Conor and all of his warriors. At the coming of winter each year, let each and every one of you suffer the pain of a woman in her birth pangs. More than that," she shouted, "at your time of greatest need, when your lands are being invaded, let a sleeping sickness fall over you all and prevent you from defending your lands."'

Fedelma paused in her storytelling to allow Maeve and Ailell to digest all that she had told them. Then she continued, 'This curse is real and each winter, the warriors suffer the pains of a woman in childbirth. They are not capable of defending their province during these times but fortunately for them, they have never had reason to fear an invasion.

'Even the king is useless during this time. Conor pretends to ignore the curse, knowing there is no cure. He refuses to mention it and has become more removed and aloof from his men. There are those who say that he rules his kingdom unfairly, looking only to amass great wealth for himself.

'Shortly after Macha placed the curse on the warriors of Ulster, Fergus decided to leave Conor's court because he disagreed with the way that the king was ruling the province. He came to Connacht and has pledged to protect and defend his new homeland. Ulster sorely misses Fergus, for he is one of the finest warriors in the land.'

Fedelma's story was complete, but her thoughts ran on. Silently, she gazed at the flickering flames of the fire, but in her mind was a picture of a young Ulster warrior, part human, part god, and an indestructible young man.

'Why do you frown so, Fedelma?' the queen interrupted her thoughts.

Fedelma awoke from her reverie and decided that the time was not appropriate to reveal what she had seen in the flames.

'Just dreaming, Your Majesty,' replied Fedelma, 'my story has tired me. May I leave now?'

'Not yet,' answered Maeve, 'tell me what you know of the two great bulls.'

'Ah, that is a very old story,' said Fedelma, and she began to tell it. 'Those two bulls are not of this world, nor are they now in the shape in which they were born. They began their lives as royal pig-keepers in the Land of the Sidhe. One pig-keeper worked for the Faery king of Connacht and the other for the Faery king of Ulster. There was bad blood between the two kings, but the pig-keepers were the best of friends. They would often visit each other and bring their pigs with them. These pig-keepers were famous, as they were skilled in the art of shape changing. The people of Connacht boasted that their pig-keeper had greater powers than the other one, while in Ulster they said that it was theirs had the greater power. That these two pig-keepers should be such good friends only heightened the dispute between the kings and finally both pig-keepers were dismissed from their work.

'They changed themselves into birds of prey and spent two years together in this shape. They spent the first year in Connacht and the second year in Ulster. During that time together, their only aim was for one to prove himself better that the other.

'At the end of two years, they changed themselves into water creatures. One went into the river Shannon and the other into the river Suir and they spent two full years under water. One year they were seen devouring each other in the Suir, the next in the Shannon. After that they became stags, and destroyed each other's dwelling places. Then they became two warriors, slashing each other. Two spirits of the air, was their next transformation, frightening each other.

'Then they became two fierce dragons and tried to destroy each other's lands with their fiery breath. Lastly, they came down onto the earth as two white maggots. One of them got into a stream up in Ulster where a cow belonging to Dara Mac Fiachna swallowed it up. The other got into a stream in Connacht and was swallowed by a cow belonging to Queen Maeve and King Ailell. From them sprang the two bulls, Finnbennach of the White Horns and the Brown Bull of Cooley. It seems to me that these two bulls are destined to cause destruction between Connacht and Ulster.'

Fedelma felt weary after her story. She had a vision of the destruction of Maeve's army by the Ulstermen, but decided to keep it to herself for now and not to risk making the queen angry.

After Fedelma left, Maeve remained deep in thought, staring at the dying embers in the fireplace. Finally she roused herself and turned to speak with her husband. There lay Ailell, sprawled in his chair, fast asleep. Maeve punched him in the side with her fist.

'Ouch!' he roared and leaped off the chair. 'What's the matter?'

Maeve glared at him, 'did you hear any of that story that Fedelma told us?'

'Of course, I did,' answered Ailell angrily, 'I only fell asleep a moment ago.'

Maeve did not really care whether he had heard or not as it was she who always made the important decisions.

'It seems to me that the time is right for us to invade Ulster,' said Maeve. 'Winter is approaching and Conor and his warriors will feel the recurrence of Macha's spell. Now Fedelma has told us that when their province is being invaded, their curse will be increased and a sleeping sickness will overtake them. So, in their time of greatest need, they will be useless against our army. Let us gather our forces and prepare to overthrow Ulster!'

Then Maeve sent word to all the men of Erin to ally themselves with her. She promised them riches in return for their fealty. Daily, they began to arrive from all over the country and their numbers swelled for this great invasion of Ulster. Her spies combed the Ulster countryside and reported back to her that all the warriors of the Red Branch were stricken in their spell sickness.

But Maeve's wise men and druids warned of danger – an unknown force that could not be defeated. Ailell heeded their warnings and wanted to postpone this invasion. After all, he himself had not much interest in war and saw no reason to invade Ulster.

'Nonsense,' said Maeve, and she sent for Fedelma again, for she had great faith in the girl's prophecies.

'I need good tidings, can you show them to me,' she asked the girl.

But Fedelma shook her head, then cast her eyes downward. The time had come for her to admit that she had seen a vision of Connacht's defeat. 'I see a young man who will be very dangerous to your majesty. He will destroy your army and kill your champions,' she said this quietly for she was afraid of the wrath of the queen.

Sure enough, Maeve leaped from her throne, screaming, 'how can this be true? My spies tell me that Conor and his warriors are stricken in pain. You are mistaken, you must be.'

But Fedelma was not mistaken, for Cúchulainn was the only Ulster warrior who did not fall under the curse of Macha and was not afflicted by the sickness. For this reason even the men of the Red Branch looked on him with awe and all wondered at the lad's immunity. They did not realise that Cúchulainn was the son of the god Lugh and so had inherited many special powers of which even he himself was unaware.

Maeve delayed her attack on Ulster until her spies brought her reports that the sleeping sickness had overcome the Ulster warriors and they could not be roused. No Connacht man knew that young Cúchulainn was still awake. Then Maeve herself decided that the time of invasion had arrived. She would ignore the signs of foreboding. Ailell would go along with her decision.

Dressing herself in her armour, she climbed into her chariot. Her fair hair hung in a long braid down her back. With her sword held high in the air, she herself went to the head of this great army and began to lead the Men of Erin into Ulster.

Cúchulainn keeps the Gap of the North

Fergus Mac Roy was a huge man – it was said that he had the strength of seven men. It was a sad day for Cúchulainn when Fergus left Ulster, as he looked on him as a father. It was Fergus who had found him by the river when he was a tiny baby and Fergus had kept an eye on the young lad as he grew up and became a warrior.

Fergus had abandoned Conor's court long before Cúchulainn was declared the champion of Ireland. Now Queen Maeve sent for him again as soon as the troops were ready to march.

'You will be my chief scout on this attack, Mac Roy,' she said haughtily, 'you know the path.'

Fergus was unwilling to lead Maeve's army against his homeland, but he could not disobey a direct order. He went ahead of the army to show the path into Ulster. But the closer he came to his homeland, the less he wanted to complete this journey. He began to lead the troops across the bog and through the briars and brambles until they were worn out. Fergus tried to send secret messages to Cúchulainn telling him of Maeve's coming.

She realised at the end of the first day that they had not made much progress and she sent for Fergus and asked him to explain.

'I will not lead your army against my province. You must find another guide to lead your troops.'

Emer brought the news of the invasion to Cúchulainn. The women at Eamhain Macha were full of news; they were out and about and had much to do while their husbands were in their sleeping sickness. They were told the news of the marching of the Men of Erin and hurried to bring the word to Cúchulainn. He called for his chariot to be made ready.

'I will go to the border between Ulster and Connacht and I shall take my stand at the Gap of the North and not allow the Men of Erin to march into Ulster. Maeve will regret her decision to attack us.'

He summoned Laeg, his charioteer, and told him to get the chariot and his horse, the Grey of Macha, the swiftest horse in the land. They drove until they found the tracks of Maeve's army. Cúchulainn went into the woods and waited until two of Maeve's chariots crept up with scouts aboard. Suddenly, Cúchulainn leapt from a tree and quick as a flash, he cut the heads off the four scouts. Then placing the headless bodies back in the chariot, he turned the chariot around and sent the horses galloping back to Maeve's camp.

The queen herself saw the chariots arrive with the bloody, headless bodies. She did not admit how much this startled her and ordered her army to march on. Later, as they rounded a bend in the path, they discovered the heads of the scouts stuck up on poles in the middle of a lake. Blood from the gory heads dripped into the lake and turned the water red.

Maeve thought that this must be the work of a band of Ulster warriors. She feared that they might be creeping up on her army so she sent for Fergus to explain.

'This is the work of the warrior Cúchulainn. He alone is taking a stand to defend Ulster,' said Fergus.

Maeve refused to believe that one warrior could have killed four of her soldiers at one time.

'But he is no ordinary warrior,' said Fergus. 'His strength and skill in war is greater than any other man. He will prove this to you if he has not already convinced you by his actions here.'

Then Maeve thought of the prophecy of Fedelma, and began to wonder if there was truth in what she had been told. She cast the thought from her mind and ordered her army to keep marching on into Ulster.

For days they pressed on through rough country, but no matter how quickly they marched, Cúchulainn always seemed to be ahead of them, waiting to kill the scouts who went ahead. Sometimes he might be on their right side, then on their left, picking off the soldiers in twos or threes with his sling shot. The soldiers never once caught a glimpse of Cúchulainn, yet day and night they heard the whistle of the stones from his sling as he harassed the Men of Erin.

The winter was very harsh that year and the winds howled in their ears as they marched. Snow fell heavily and at times reached to the hubs of the chariot wheels. Many times the wheels of the chariots had to be dug out before the journey could continue. The soldiers were terrified. At night, when they camped, they found no rest. The sound of stones from Cúchulainn's sling-shot whistled through the air throughout the night and in the morning, many were found dead on the ground.

Finally, the scouts were so frightened that they

refused to leave camp unless in a very large group. Maeve herself grew nervous and met with Ailell and the captains of war. They had no answers or suggestions as none had yet seen the face of the enemy.

'Could it be true that we are being attacked by only one man?' asked Ailell in amazement.

Maeve decided to send for Fergus once again to explain. He came to the tent and told them the story of how Setanta had been found by the magical river Boyne when he was just a baby. 'Nobody knows for certain from whence this child came,' explained Fergus, 'but he is from Faeryland and many believe that he is the son of a god.'

Silence settled in Maeve's tent, no one doubted that there could be truth in these words. Fergus went on to tell them how young Setanta had earned his name when he killed the fierce wolfhound. He told them of his warrior training and how he had won the title of 'champion of Ireland'.

When Fergus finished his story, Maeve dismissed all the men from her tent and sat pondering the situation. She was now very curious to meet Cúchulainn and sent her messengers to find him. It was night time and the terrified messengers could not be sure where Cúchulainn was hiding. They called out loudly as they walked, explaining that they brought a message from their queen.

Cúchulainn called to them from high up in a tree where he had concealed himself. 'Tell your queen that I will meet her after dawn tomorrow, in the glen near where you are now camped.'

The next morning, one hour after sunrise, Maeve and Ailell went to the glen and found Cúchulainn already there standing on a hill. They went and stood on the opposite hill so that they might have the glen between them. Then Maeve sent her messengers with words of flattery to Cúchulainn. She promised him lands and riches if he would come over to her side and abandon Ulster. Cúchulainn at once sent back a refusal and immediately left the glen.

All that day and night he continued his attack on the Men of Erin. This pattern continued in the days that followed and Maeve's army knew no rest.

One day, Maeve was walking outside her tent with her pet raven perched on one shoulder and her pet squirrel on the other. Suddenly a stone whistled by and Maeve's bird fell dead to the ground. She began to run as fast as she could for the safety of her tent. But before she could reach it, another stone whistled by and killed her pet squirrel. Terrified, Maeve sent for Fergus and told him to go to Cúchulainn and ask what terms he would accept.

When Cúchulainn saw Fergus approach, he went out to meet him. They embraced each other and they were joyful at the meeting. Cúchulainn welcomed Fergus into his tent and sent Laeg, his charioteer, to bring food and drink for them. Then Fergus explained his reason for coming and asked Cúchulainn what terms he would accept to allow the Men of Erin to rest at night and not fear his secret attacks.

'Tell Maeve that she should not advance into Ulster by forced marches, but rather she should send one of her best warriors to fight me in single combat each day. While the combat is taking place, the armies may march on, but once the soldier is killed, the marching should halt until the next day.'

Fergus said that he would take this message back to Maeve. He then took his leave of Cúchulainn and they both were very sad at the parting for they had lived like father and son for so many years together in Ulster, and they loved each other dearly.

That night, Cúchulainn returned home to spend the evening with Emer. It was three months since he had left home to defend the Gap of the North and he had sorely missed her. In all that time, he had never had a full night's rest, catching quick naps between his attacks on the Men of Erin. Emer had worried for his safety, although Cúchulainn sent her frequent messages to assure her that he was well.

Emer thought her husband looked sad as if he carried the weight of the world on his shoulders. They sat together in front of a raging fire and a harpist played soothing music while Emer sang for Cúchulainn. He fell asleep in her arms but rose before dawn and returned to guard Ulster at the Gap of the North.

Maeve agreed to Cúchulainn's terms, thinking that it would be better to lose one man each day rather than one hundred, 'even,' she said, 'if that one man be a champion.'

At first Maeve kept to the bargain and sent one warrior at a time to fight against Cúchulainn. Her army advanced while the battle took place. But even the finest of her soldiers could last only a very short time against Cúchulainn and her army made little progress in a day. She soon changed her tune and sent one warrior after another to fight Cúchulainn. As soon as one fell, another took his place so that Cúchulainn had no rest from morning till night, but he remained undefeated. Finally she sent one hundred warriors all at once to fight him. The struggle was fierce, but Cúchulainn killed them all in twos and threes and the bodies piled high in the ford, across the gap. That night, he sat by the campfire that Laeg had prepared for him on a hill overlooking the camp of the Men of Erin. Exhausted and wounded, Cúchulainn rested his head on his knees. Laeg called to him that a stranger was approaching, alone and on foot.

'What manner of person is he?' asked Cúchulainn.

'He is tall and stately and carries himself like a god. He wears a purple cloak fastened with a brooch of gold imbedded with diamonds,' Laeg replied. 'He is walking through the great camp as if invisible for no man is taking notice of him.'

'It may be some god or man from Faeryland who is coming to comfort me,' said Cúchulainn.

Suddenly Cúchulainn was surrounded by sweet music and the tall stranger approached quietly and smiling at Cúchulainn he said: 'sleep now, my son, and in your sleep I will heal your wounds.'

It was Lugh of the Long Arm, god of the sun and the harvest who had come from Faeryland to heal the champion. He began to sing and soon Cúchulainn fell into a deep sleep. When he awoke, late next morning, he was alone with his charioteer, but his wounds were healed and he felt well rested.

He arose and looked down at the army gathered below, ready to march. Cúchulainn quickly slipped through the woods with his weapons and, from dawn till dark, he again halted the advances of Maeve's army by killing her warriors one after another.

That evening, Maeve sat with Ailell in their tent, bemoaning the loss of so many men. 'What is worse, is that we have made so little progress into Ulster. This should be an opportune time for us to invade with the Red Branch warriors in their sickness spell.'

She paced back and forth then sent for Fergus Mac Roy.

As soon as he entered, she began pleading with him, 'you must fight against Cúchulainn, there is no other warrior who is capable.'

'Never,' shouted Fergus in reply, 'I will never do battle against him.'

When her pleads went unheeded Maeve resorted to orders, 'you are in service to me now and must obey my commands. I can turn the men of Ulster out of my army as quickly as I please.'

Many of the Red Branch warriors had left Ulster with Fergus and joined Maeve's army. Fergus did not wish them to lose their jobs and so was finally persuaded to fight in single combat with Cúchulainn.

The following morning, Cúchulainn was surprised to see Fergus approach the Gap of the North. 'Surely you do not come to fight me, unarmed,' Cúchulainn called out.

'I would not fight you even if I had my sword,' replied Fergus. 'I come to ask you to retreat from me.'

Cúchulainn scoffed. 'I have never retreated from a fight and will not do so from you. Why would you ask this of me?'

'Because there is a great love between us. I have

no wish to fight you. but I cannot break a bond with the queen of Connacht. If you retreat from me now, I guarantee that in the final battle between the Men of Erin and the Ulstermen I will run from your sword and Ulster will be victorious.'

Cúchulainn agreed to this bargain and turned and walked into the forest. Fergus returned to Maeve and as he approached, she called out, 'go back, follow him, don't let him get away.'

'I will not hunt down my friend,' Fergus replied. Then Maeve sent a group of her warriors in pursuit. They ran together into the woods. Moments later, Cúchulainn appeared and they fought. Very soon, the warriors lay dead at his feet. Maeve tried to persuade more of her soldiers to follow Cúchulainn, but none would agree to go, they were terrified.

Angrily, Maeve stormed off to her tent calling for Ailell and her captains of war. When all were assembled, they found her pacing up and down in her tent, shouting and wringing her hands, 'have we no soldier in our ranks who is the equal of this Cúchulainn? Surely we must have someone who is as strong and skilled and as brave as this man?'

'There is someone, Your Majesty,' answered

one of her captains. 'He is Ferdia, son of Daman, a Fir Bolg chieftain. He and Cúchulainn were boyhood friends in training across the sea in Alba. It is said that the woman warrior, Scatha, never had the equal of these boys when they trained at her warrior school in the Land of Shadows. It will be difficult to persuade him to fight Cúchulainn, they swore eternal friendship to each other.'

'I will be the judge of that,' snapped Maeve, 'send for Ferdia.'

Very reluctantly, Ferdia came to Maeve's tent, for he knew what she wanted of him. Maeve flattered him and offered him land and riches if he would fight against Cúchulainn. Her servants brought wine and she refilled Ferdia's goblet several times.

'I have heard of your skill and bravery as a warrior, Ferdia. I believe that you can defeat Cúchulainn.'

'I love my friend. I will never fight against him.'

Maeve now knew that her flatteries and bribes would not break the bond of friendship between Cúchulainn and Ferdia.

'It seems to me, Ferdia, that Cúchulainn was telling me the truth about you.'

'What do you mean, what did Cúchulainn say about me?' asked Ferdia.

'He said that he could easily defeat you in combat.'

Ferdia jumped to his feet. 'Cúchulainn had no right to say such a thing. I swear I will be the first to fight him at dawn tomorrow.'

Ferdia went away to rest, with his eyes downcast. He was filled with shame, knowing that Maeve had tricked him. She had extorted that pledge from him while he was under the influence of wine.

At dawn the next morning, Cúchulainn was shocked to see Ferdia approach the hillside with his weapons in hand.

'Surely you have not come to fight me, my friend?' asked Cúchulainn.

Ferdia hung his head and explained, 'Maeve tricked me into believing your boast that you could defeat me. But I cannot break my bond, now that it is given. I would be shamed before all. I am sorry for allowing myself to be tricked.'

'How can I fight you Ferdia, when I love you like a brother? This fighting has to stop!'

'But Cúchulainn, our friendship means nothing to those we serve. They care only for power and possessions. We fight only to obey their commands.'

The fighting began at the Gap of the North and was long and fierce, each warrior a perfect match for the other. They changed their weapons from time to time and so skilled were they both that neither warrior had even the smallest wound when at nightfall they agreed to stop the combat for that day. They embraced, but did not rest at the same campfire. Instead, they each went to their own hillside where their charioteers had set camps. They sent each other food and drink and messengers from fairy dwellings brought herbs and potions for Cúchulainn's aching limbs. These he shared, each and every one, with Ferdia.

The following morning, they took up their weapons again and the fighting resumed. All day long the fighting was long and hard and, on this day, both warriors received many wounds. They laid down their weapons at dusk and again they embraced before going to rest on separate hills. As they lay exhausted, their charioteers shared the same fire and their horses were put out in the one paddock together.

The next morning, Cúchulainn noticed a great change in his friend. Ferdia's eyes were downcast and a great weight of worry creased his brow. Cú-chulainn walked across the ford to greet him and asked Ferdia to call off the fight.

'I cannot break my vow to the queen,' answered Ferdia. 'Let the fight begin.'

All day long the struggle continued and at day's end they were both so sorely wounded and exhausted that they dropped their weapons in the spot where they stopped fighting and dragged their feet to their camps. That night there was no communication between the camps and both warriors slept wearily until dawn.

Next day when the fighting resumed both warriors knew that there would be an end to it this day. Ferdia had dressed in his battle suit made from thick hides. He knew he would need to protect himself from Cúchulainn's deadly weapon, the Ga Bolga. This barbed spear was thrown with the foot and could pierce every part of its victim's body. All day long, they struggled fiercely, swords clashing noisily on shields. As evening approached, Ferdia managed to sink his sword into Cúchulainn's chest, right up to the hilt. The blood flowed so freely that it reddened the water in the ford. Before Cúchulainn could recover, Ferdia stabbed him twice more.

With his remaining strength, Cúchulainn reached for the Ga Bolga and just before he collapsed, he threw it with his foot. The deadly barbs pierced Ferdia's entire body. He reeled backward from the blow, then fell dead into the ford.

Cúchulainn quickly climbed down into the water and picked up his friend's body. He carried it to the hillside and placed it gently on the ground. Then Cúchulainn knelt down and cried aloud over the loss of his friend.

'Why did this have to happen?' he called to the sky, but received no reply.

The charioteers kept their distance until the sound of Cúchulainn's sobs abated. Then Laeg advised Cúchulainn to leave the area immediately, lest Maeve, in a rage, should send a hundred warriors at once to avenge Ferdia's death.

Ulster Awakes

After the fight with Ferdia, Cúchulainn lay on the ground sorely wounded in body and spirit. Laeg, his charioteer, brought him to the hillside and laid him on the ground to rest. He had no strength left to withstand the advances and attacks of Maeve's army. As he lay there, Sualdam, his foster-father, heard of his condition and came to see if he could help him. He was horrified to find Cúchulainn covered in wounds and badly bruised all over his body. He began to wail and lament, but Cúchulainn quickly stopped him and told him to go at once to King Conor's court at Eamhain Macha and urge the Red Branch warriors to awaken and save their lands from invasion. Sualdam immediately jumped on his horse and galloped away to Eamhain Macha.

When Sualdam arrived at the court, all was quiet. He rode all around the building shouting at the top of his voice 'Wake up, men of Ulster, arise and save your lands.' Inside, the warriors lay sleeping, and were not disturbed by the shouting. In a rage, Sualdam rode his horse into the great hall, shouting and urging the warriors to wake up. They lay stretched out, sleeping on the floor. Sualdam was so angry when he could not waken them that he turned his horse around to gallop out of the building. But he pulled on the reins furiously and his horse reared up. Sualdam's head was thrown onto his shield and the sharp rim cut his head clean off his body. The headless body lay across the horse's neck as he galloped away.

From where it lay on the ground, Sualdam's head continued to call out to the warriors: 'Arise, men of Ulster, arise and save your lands.'

Finally, some of the warriors began to stir. Conor himself opened his eyes and called, 'who is shouting? Keep quiet, we want to sleep.' But still the head kept calling. After many hours, the king arose and realising what was happening he began to waken his warriors. 'Get up, quickly,' he called, 'our lands are being invaded. We have been in a sleeping spell.' His men woke up, grabbed their weapons and rushed to their horses. They jumped on their horses and set off at great speed for the Gap of the North.

Meanwhile, Cúchulainn awoke on the hill and saw Laeg standing anxiously over him.

'Why do you look so worried, my faithful friend?' Cúchulainn asked.

'You are so weak and wounded, I feared for your life, but now I worry that the army of our enemies will succeed in invading Ulster. Maeve knows of your injuries, I saw her spies close by during the night. They have brought her news that you can no longer defend Ulster single-handedly and her troops are lining up for a huge attack.'

'Help me to rise, and put my spear and my shield in my hand,' said Cúchulainn.

'But you are not able to hold off their advances any longer,' protested Laeg.

'I must do all that I can, even if it means the loss of my own life. Help me now to go and stand in the ford.'

Laeg knew that it was useless to protest. Nevertheless he tried to prevent Cúchulainn from attempting to stand alone against the great force of the Men of Erin. 'I will go with you and fight beside you as long as there is blood flowing in my veins,' said Laeg.

Cúchulainn did not argue but was thinking that the end might be very close. For a brief moment an image of Emer flashed before him, her sad eyes beseeching him to take care.

As the two men walked slowly down to the ford, they heard shouts from the other side of the hill and the thundering sound of galloping hooves. Suddenly over the hilltop rode King Conor, leading his Red Branch warriors to defend Ulster.

As swiftly as he could, Laeg forced Cúchulainn to a sheltered place near a cluster of large rocks. There Laeg beckoned for help to a group of the Red Branch warriors. As gently but forcibly as they could, the men tied Cúchulainn to one of the rocks and refused to allow him to join in the battle. They explained to him that they were doing this for his own good. Cúchulainn's attempts to escape were in vain and he was too weak to struggle for long.

The Ulster warriors were numerous and fierce in their desire to revenge themselves on the Men of Erin. Maeve's army was confused and surprised by the sudden attack. The queen herself jumped in her chariot and led them onward, trying to drive back the men of Ulster. Three times they succeeded but finally, in a great surge, the Ulster warriors sent the Connacht men into retreat. Ailell was one of the first to seek shelter from the battle, realising that all was lost.

King Conor rushed to attack a group of Connacht men and found himself facing Fergus Mac Roy, now his bitterest enemy, whose throne he had taken. Fergus raised up his great sword and it clashed against Conor's shield. This was a magical shield and it cried out whenever Conor was in danger. When Cúchulainn heard its cries, he tore himself loose from his bindings and jumped to his feet. Seizing his weapons, he ran toward the sound of the wailing shield and was just in time to see Fergus raise up his sword again with both hands and prepare to strike Conor a death blow. Cúchulainn jumped between them, shouting, 'fight me instead, Fergus.'

As Fergus lowered his sword, the king retreated swiftly and joined some of his warriors who were putting the Men of Erin to flight on the other side of the ford.

Fergus glared angrily at Cúchulainn for he felt that Conor deserved to die.

'I am bound to defend my province and my king,' said Cúchulainn, knowing how Fergus felt.

'That king does not deserve your bravery and loyalty, Cúchulainn.'

Cúchulainn reminded Fergus of his promise to

retreat from him on the day of the great battle.

'For I retreated from you when you were sent by your queen to fight against me.'

Fergus looked on Cúchulainn with fatherly love and he was sad so see the young man so badly wounded but yet so determined to defend his province. 'It is with a heavy heart that I turn from you for I know not when you and I will meet again. But I will keep my promise and retreat.'

As Fergus pretended to flee from Cúchulainn, a large band of soldiers from Maeve's army followed. If Fergus, one of their greatest warriors, was giving up the fight, they thought that it would be useless to continue. Seeing all of these warriors retreating the Men of Erin suddenly broke their ranks and ran from the attack of the Ulstermen. Over the hill and westward they ran and did not stop until they were sure that the Ulstermen no longer pursued them. Then they slowed to a march but continued on their journey homeward.

When Maeve realised that the she had lost the battle, she drew aside some of her soldiers and secretly sent them on into Ulster to Cooley. She instructed them not to return without Dara Mac Fiachna's Brown Bull. The men easily found Dara's house and there, in the paddock adjoining was the great Brown Bull of Cooley. They waited until the dead of night, then, as quietly as possible, the messengers put a halter on the bull with a long length of rope attached and led him away from the paddock. All through the night they journeyed south-westward and by morning they were close to the place where the defeated army of Maeve had camped for the night.

Maeve was on the look-out and when she saw her messengers arrive with the great Brown Bull of Cooley a smile spread over her face and a feeling of triumph raised her spirits. This great bull, after all was the reason for the invasion of Ulster and did she not now have what she had set out to take by force? Maeve herself roused her soldiers and sent them on their way back to Connacht. Not a word of thanks or gratitude did she give them to take on their long return journey. Not a man amongst them had a good thought for his queen as they marched wearily homeward.

Maeve sent the men with the bull on ahead of the army and she herself accompanied them in her chariot. Ailell had already returned home to Cruachan. He had lost all interest in the battle when he realised that there was no hope of victory and, placing Fergus Mac Roy in charge of his men, he had abandoned them and set off for home. Now his servants alerted him that his wife had returned. She herself came to seek him, calling out, 'Ailell, my husband, I have something to show you.' She found him in the throne room and called him to look out the window. Below in his paddock was Finnbennach, Ailell's beautiful white-horned bull. But now also in the paddock was the new bull, the Brown Bull of Cooley!

Ailell looked in astonishment as Maeve gloated, 'you see, now we are equal in our possessions. I have brought this fine bull home to add to my herd.'

Suddenly, they heard the snorting of the bulls and as they watched, the two bulls began to stomp the ground with their huge hooves. Great clumps of earth were sent flying skyward. The bulls' eyes blazed as they glared at each other, then they dropped their heads and charged. The sound of their heads banging together was like a great clap of thunder. They began to slash and gore each other as they chased around the paddock. Then Finnbennach, the White-Horned, managed to sink

his horns into the side of the Brown Bull but the Brown Bull pulled away and came charging back at Finnbennach. This time the Brown Bull sunk his horns so deep into the side of the White-Horned bull that he was pushed across the paddock and right through the wooden fence. The Brown Bull then shook his horns and dropped the dead body of the White-Horned Bull at his feet. For a moment, the Brown Bull looked down on the corpse as if wondering why their long rivalry should end this way. Blood poured from the great gash in his side and he stood exhausted, breathing heavily over the body of the dead bull. Then he raised his head and looked all around. His gaze found the horrified faces of the king and queen in the window above and he looked at them for a moment. But his strength was fading fast, and a moment later, the Brown Bull lay dead beside the body of the White-Horned Bull.

Once again, Maeve and Ailell were equal in their possessions and as usual, neither was content. Maeve felt no remorse about the war she had started and the lives that were lost. Her only regret was that she did not have the Brown Bull in her possession. She would have liked to make him obey her!

Epilogue

Peace had come at last!

At Eamhain Macha, the victory celebrations lasted for seven days and seven nights. Bonfires were lit each evening and men, women and children danced on the hillside, long into the night.

King Conor realised what a great debt Ulster owed to its hero and he bestowed many gifts on Cúchulainn. He gave him large tracts of the best land in Ulster, a herd of cattle and sacks filled with gold.

Cúchulainn's strength quickly returned with Emer's care. Each evening she sang sweet lullabies for him, as he drifted into sleep. The sound of her song was there to welcome him when he arose in the morning. He had missed her so much during those lonely months when he was forced to be parted from her and his heart rejoiced to be close to her again.

As summer approached, Cúchulainn often walked on the seashore and found his thoughts wandering over the sea. Sometimes, old Cathbad accompanied him, leaning on a stick as he walked along. The druid had already lived the life span of three men and knew that he had not many more days left on earth. He liked to spend his time in the company of Cúchulainn, passing on the old stories and teaching him to read the stars.

One evening, late in the summer as they strolled on the beach near Dún Dealgan, they saw a small boat approach swiftly across the waves. Two figures, a man and a woman, stood in the boat, both tall and slender. They wore fine silk cloaks fastened with gold brooches and their stature was like that of gods. Cúchulainn went to help them pull their boat up on the sand and he knew immediately that this was the man who had come from Tír na nÓg to comfort and heal him when he was wounded in battle. The woman had long red hair and she looked lovingly at Cúchulainn. 'My son, we have watched over you since we sent you from Faeryland when you were an infant. We are glad to see you well.'

Cúchulainn was astonished by what she said, but she continued, 'I am Dechtera, your mother, and this is your father Lugh. He came to comfort you when you were wounded in battle.'

Dechtera turned to Cathbad. The druid had

been staring, speechless, since the boat landed. A smile spread across her face and she ran to embrace the old man. 'Father,' she whispered as he hugged her to him. 'Father, it is time for you to come with us. We have come to bring you to Tír na nÓg.' Dechtera took her father's hands in hers and gave them a squeeze.

Tears of joy ran silently down the old druid's cheeks. 'I have always hoped and longed for this moment to arrive, but was never certain that it would. Your husband is a fine man, and your son is Ulster's hero.'

Cúchulainn now understood that he was the son of Cathbad's long lost daughter, Dechtera, and his father was the god, Lugh! He was pleased and proud to have finally discovered his ancestry.

These four stayed talking on the beach for a long time that day. Dechtera explained that after she went to live in Tír na nÓg, she knew that her father was lonely without her. So she and Lugh decided to send their son to be raised under his watchful eye. Now in his great old age, it was time for Cathbad to return with them to Tír na nÓg.

When the time came for them to leave, his parents and his grandfather embraced Cúchulainn and then he helped Cathbad aboard the boat. He watched as the waves carried the boat away from him but knew that his family would be watching over him from afar. He turned and walked back home to Emer.

FAVOURITE IRISH LEGENDS
A Dual Language Book

BAIRBRE MCCARTHY

Favourite Irish Legends includes three of the most famous Irish legends in English with parallel text in Irish. 'The Children of Lir' ('Leanaí Lir') is accompanied by 'Balor of the Evil Eye' ('Balor Drochshúile') and the beautiful tragic 'Wooing of Etáin' ('Tóraíocht Etáin'). The book is a unique introduction to the legends, bringing them to life both in English and Irish.

IRISH LEPRECHAUN STORIES

BAIRBRE MCCARTHY

The leprechaun is the keeper of the crock of gold at the end of the rainbow and he knows where all the wealth of the world is buried. If you are lucky enough to catch him, you must keep your eyes on him at all times and not allow him to distract your attention or he will disappear. If he does not outsmart you he can make you very wealthy and make your wishes come true!

Stories of Old Ireland for Children

Eddie Lenihan

Long ago in Ireland there were men who used to travel to the four corners of the earth and few travelled farther than Fionn and the men of the Fianna during their many adventures. In *Stories of Old Ireland for Children* we read about 'Fionn MacCumhail and the Feathers from China', 'King Cormac's Fighting Academy' and 'Fionn and the Mermaids'.

Enchanted Irish Tales

Patricia Lynch

Enchanted Irish Tales tells of ancient heroes and heroines, fantastic deeds of bravery, magical kingdoms, weird and wonderful animals. This illustrated edition of classical folktales, retold by Patricia Lynch with all the imagination and warmth for which she is renowned, rekindles the age-old legends of Ireland, as exciting today as they were when first told. This collection includes: Conary Mór and the Three Red Riders, The Long Life of Tuan MacCarrell, Finn Mac-Cool and the Fianna, Oisín and the Land of Youth, The Kingdom of the Dwarfs, The Dragon Ring of Connla, Mac Datho's Boar and Ethne.